# The Knightly Campout

adapted by Cordelia Evans

based on the screenplay written by Simon Nicholson

Ready-to-Read

Simon Spotlight

New York  London  Toronto  Sydney  New Delhi

SIMON SPOTLIGHT

An imprint of Simon & Schuster Children's Publishing Division

1230 Avenue of the Americas, New York, New York 10020

For information about special discounts for bulk purchases, please contact Simon & Schuster Special Sales at 1-866-506-1949 or business@simonandschuster.com.

Manufactured in the United States of America 0414 LAK

First Edition 10 9 8 7 6 5 4 3 2 1

ISBN 978-1-4814-0418-1 (pbk)

ISBN 978-1-4814-0419-8 (hc)

ISBN  978-1-4814-0420-4 (eBook)

Sparkie and Squirt were taking a nap.

Mike decided he wanted to do something knightly.

Their nap gave him an idea!

Mike woke up the dragons.
"I want to camp overnight
in the Tall Tree Woods!"
he said.

Mike hopped on Galahad.
He reached for his sword
and pulled out a cup of . . .

"Hot chocolate?" asked
Sparkie.

"I will not need that on my
campout," said Mike.

Squirt had a list of things that Mike would need. But Mike said he was going to camp with nothing. That was the knightly way!

Mike tried to build
a tent out of sticks.

But it fell down.

Finally, he got it to stay.

Then he saw that Sparkie and Squirt had a big tent to sleep in.

Mike gathered more sticks

to make a bed.

It was not comfy.

Squirt got out his bed.

It was very comfy!

"Do you want a blanket,

Mike?" asked Squirt.

"No, thank you," said Mike.

"I am camping out

the knightly way."

Then the dragons made campout stew.

"Mike, we have some stew for you!" said Squirt.

"No, thank you," said Mike.

"I will eat an apple.

That is the knightly way!"

But Mike could not reach

the apples.

"Here is a box to stand on!"

said Squirt.

"Here is a ladder!"

said Sparkie.

"No, thank you," said Mike.

"I will stand on this lump."

But the lump was an anthill!

Mike ran around to get the

ants off.

Mike bumped into his tent.

It came crashing down.

"Oh no!" said Mike. "I wanted to do things the knightly way, with no help!"

"It is okay if we help,"

said Sparkie.

"As long as you sleep outside all night, you are still knightly!"

"I guess you are right," said Mike.

The dragons helped Mike fix his tent and gave him stew.

Mike shared his hot
chocolate.

Then they all went to bed.
They slept outside all night.
It was the perfect knightly
campout!